24 /5/21

Look out for:

The Lonely Lion Cub
The Puzzled Penguin
The Playful Panda
The Silky Seal Pup
The Eager Elephant
The Lucky Snow Leopard
The Pesky Polar Bear
The Cuddly Koala
The Wild Wolf Pup
The Happy Hippo
The Sleepy Snowy Owl
The Scruffy Sea Otter
The Picky Puffin
The Giggly Giraffe
The Curious Kangaroo
The Super Sloth
The Little Llama
The Messy Meerkat
The Helpful Hedgehog

Zoe's Rescue Zoo

The Rowdy Red Panda

Amelia Cobb

Illustrated by
Sophy Williams

nosy
crow

With special thanks to Siobhan Curham

For Sadie Hardin

First published in the UK in 2021 by Nosy Crow Ltd
The Crow's Nest, 14 Baden Place
Crosby Row, London SE1 1YW

www.nosycrow.com

ISBN: 978 1 78800 933 1

Nosy Crow and associated logos are trademarks and/or
registered trademarks of Nosy Crow Ltd

Text copyright © Working Partners Ltd, 2021
Illustrations © Sophy Williams, 2021

The right of Working Partners Ltd and Sophy Williams to be identified as the author
and illustrator respectively of this work has been asserted asserted by them in accordance with
the Copyright, Designs and Patents Act 1988.

A CIP catalogue record for this book will be available from the British Library

Printed and bound in Great Britain by Clays Ltd, Elcograf S.p.A.

Papers used by Nosy Crow are made from wood grown in sustainable forests.

MIX
Paper from
responsible sources
FSC® C018072
FSC
www.fsc.org

1 3 5 7 9 10 8 6 4 2

Chapter One
Snow-Globe Zoo

Zoe Parker grinned as she stepped outside her front door. A thick blanket of snow covered the ground and a few feathery flakes drifted through the air. It was as if the Rescue Zoo where she lived had turned into a snow globe overnight! Zoe's grey mouse lemur, Meep, scampered ahead, leaving a trail of tiny paw prints

1

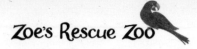

in the snow.

"Wait for me!" called Zoe, as Meep leapt over the garden gate. It was still early on Saturday morning, and the zoo hadn't opened yet. The only footprints were from the keepers, on their way to feed the animals their breakfast.

"What does snow taste like?" asked Meep, scooping up a pawful.

Zoe was able to understand what he was saying because she had a special secret – she was able to talk to animals! But no-one knew her secret, not even her Great-Uncle Horace, who owned the Rescue Zoo, or her mum, Lucy, who was the zoo vet.

"It tastes like cold," Zoe giggled as she opened the gate and joined him outside.

Meep licked the snow and shivered.

"I think I prefer bananas, they're not so freezing!" He scampered back over to Zoe. She picked him up and tucked him inside her coat. Mouse lemurs were from a very hot country called Madagascar. It wasn't surprising that Meep didn't like being cold.

"Morning, Zoe!"

Zoe turned to see Valeria walking towards her. Valeria was the keeper in charge of the Rainforest Dome. Zoe knew that was the one place in the zoo that wouldn't be

cold, no matter how much snow fell. The
Rainforest Dome had to be kept extra
hot for the tropical animals and plants
that lived there.

"Hi Valeria," said Zoe. "Are you
enjoying the snow?"

"Yes, I love it," replied Valeria with a
grin. "We never get snow in Venezuela,
where I come from. It's so much fun. Are
you looking forward to the competition
tomorrow?"

"I can't wait!" Zoe said excitedly. The
next day, the zoo was taking part in
a competition called the Snowy Paws
Award, meant to choose the animal
attraction that did the best job of
encouraging guests to visit it even in cold
winter weather. The Rescue Zoo would
be competing against petting zoos, farms

that welcomed visitors, and even a bird park.

To help their cause, the Rescue Zoo had planned special exhibits of all the wintry animals, as well as a contest to see which child could build the best animal out of snow. They'd also gotten some volunteers to come and help decorate the zoo to make it look extra pretty and festive in the snow! Zoe was doing lots to help get the zoo ready too, and they were finishing up all the preparations before the judge arrived the next morning. Zoe really hoped they would win!

"Well, I'd love to stay and play in the snow but I'd better go and feed my animals breakfast," said Valeria. "Have a lovely day, Zoe."

"Let's go and see how the exhibits are

getting on," Zoe said to Meep. Hugging him close, she hurried along the path that led to the penguins' enclosure. The huge iceberg in the middle of the lagoon looked even more magical now it was covered with real snow. The penguins were all waddling around on it. They looked really happy.

"Good morning, Zoe," called Will, the penguins' keeper.

"Morning, Will," replied Zoe. "Are the penguins getting ready for the show tomorrow?"

"Oh yes, they're keeping everything tidy, and I'm planning on giving them an extra helping of krill for their breakfast in the morning so they'll have lots of energy when they're performing for the judge," Will grinned.

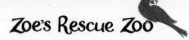

"Cool!" Krill were small fish that penguins loved to eat. Zoe knew this because she loved helping all the keepers in the zoo and learning as much about the animals as she could. When she was older, she wanted to be a zookeeper too.

"Could you put up this poster for me?" asked Will, handing it to her as he started to clean out the indoor part of the penguin enclosure.

"Sure." Zoe took the poster and hung it on the enclosure wall. "There you go, Will," she called. There were lots of fun facts about penguins on the poster. Zoe had helped Will make it the day before.

"Great, thank you!" Will called back.

"Tell me a fun penguin fact, Zoe," chirped Meep from inside her coat.

"Penguins are one of the only birds who

can't fly in the air," replied Zoe.

"Why can't they fly in the air?"

"Because they only need to fly in the sea." Zoe giggled at Meep's confused expression. "When they flap their wings in the water it helps them to swim really fast," she explained. "They have special veins in their feet to stop them from getting cold, too."

"That's what I need!" chattered Meep.

Zoe giggled as she snuggled him in tighter. "Come on, let's go and see the other winter animals."

After checking on the snow leopards, llamas, and polar bears, Zoe made her way to the café at the centre of the zoo. Sally, the café manager, was outside putting some hats, scarves and funny glasses on a table.

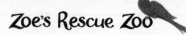

"Hi Zoe," she called. "Could you help me put out the props for the snow-animal contest?"

"Of course!" Zoe hurried inside the café and picked up a handful of hats and scarves. She couldn't wait to see the snow animals being built. The children would be using the day to explore the zoo and decide which snow animal to build before the judging the next day. Her twin cousins, Willow and Sam, were coming and they were so excited to participate. Zoe had a feeling they'd have a hard time agreeing on what animal to make – the twins argued about everything!

Zoe was looking forward to seeing the twins and her Auntie Laura, who was her mother's younger sister. She didn't get to see them very often, as they lived a few

hours away, but they happened to be
in town in time for the contest and Zoe
thought they'd really enjoy it. They were
a few years younger than Zoe and were
very sporty and competitive.

"Thanks, Zoe," said Sally as Zoe
hurried out clutching the bundle of props.
Then she looked at her watch. "We're just
in time. The gates will be opening any
minute!"

Zoe gasped. "Time to get to work!"
She hurried through the zoo. It all looked
so magical in the snow – and it would
only look better once they were done
decorating!

There was already a line of people
outside, waiting to come in. Zoe spotted
her Auntie Laura and the twins, who

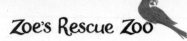

waved at her.

"There they are!" Zoe said to Meep, waving back.

"Goo! Goo!" chattered Meep.

Zoe saw that he was pointing his paw at the sky. A hot air balloon was drifting above them. Its stripes were every colour of the rainbow. "Goo!" Meep said again, bouncing up and down.

"Great-Uncle Horace!" Zoe cried. Great-Uncle Horace had rescued Meep when he was a tiny baby and because he hadn't been able to say his name properly, Meep called him Goo. Zoe and Meep weren't the only ones pleased to see the balloon. All around the zoo the animals started bellowing and roaring and chattering and squawking with excitement. Great-Uncle Horace had rescued them all, so they loved him very much.

"Do you think he's brought another rescue animal with him?" Zoe whispered to Meep. "Oh, I hope so! That would just be the perfect addition to our plan for the Snowy Paws Award!"

The zoo gates opened for the day and people hurried inside. Great-Uncle Horace leaned over the side of the balloon's basket, waving at the crowd. He was wearing a stripy scarf and hat that both perfectly matched the balloon. Perched on his shoulder was a beautiful blue bird. It was his hyacinth macaw, Kiki, who travelled everywhere with him. Zoe wondered where he had been this time. Just then, she spotted a furry white nose poking over the top of the basket. Then a

whole face
appeared. The
nose, cheeks and
ears were white but

the rest of the fur was as red as a fox.

"What kind of animal is that, Zoe?" asked Meep.

"I'm not sure." Zoe knew most animals but this was one she hadn't seen before. Then, in a flash of red fur, the animal leapt on to the edge of the basket. Everyone in the crowd gasped.

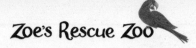

"Oh no, it's going to fall out!" exclaimed Zoe.

Just in time, Great-Uncle Horace caught the creature and scooped it into his arms. The balloon touched down and he climbed out, still holding the bundle of red fur.

"Good morning, everyone!" Great-Uncle Horace boomed. "Welcome to the Rescue Zoo. And an extra special welcome to our very latest addition – this little red panda!"

Chapter Two
Runaway Red Panda

Meep peeped out at the new arrival from inside Zoe's coat. "I thought all pandas were black and white, like Chi Chi and Mei Mei," he chattered.

"So did I," whispered Zoe, thinking of the twin panda cubs Great-Uncle Horace had rescued many months ago.

Just then, Willow and Sam came

running over.

"Hi, Zoe," they chorused, giving her a hug.

"Hi Willow. Hi Sam. Do you want to come and see the red panda?"

"Yes please," said Sam.

"She's so cute," sighed Willow.

They all hurried over to Great-Uncle Horace.

"Zoe, Willow, Sam! It's so lovely to see you!" exclaimed Great-Uncle Horace. "What do you think of our new arrival? She seems very happy to be here." The red panda wriggled and squeaked with excitement.

"She's lovely." Zoe looked at the red panda. The patches around her eyes and nose were the same as Chi Chi and Mei Mei's. But they were a brownish red and white instead of black and white. And the red panda's body was a lot smaller than a panda bear's, and a different shape. She was more like a cat than a bear, with a long fluffy tail. "Where's she from?"

"Well, originally, she's all the way from the Himalayan mountains in Asia," said Great-Uncle Horace.

"Wow!" exclaimed Sam. "That's really far away!"

"But you haven't been gone long," Zoe said. "Certainly not long enough to go all the way to Asia!"

"That's right," explained Great-Uncle Horace. "This little one was actually in a zoo nearby that's closing down. She's been living there so long that she wouldn't be able to fend for herself in the wild, so she needs a new home. Luckily, she seems to

like being around people!" He chuckled
as the red panda waved her front paws
and hooted at the crowd.

"It's like she's saying hello to us," Willow
giggled.

Zoe grinned. If only Willow knew that
was exactly what the red panda was
saying! Zoe couldn't wait to be alone
with her, so she could talk to the red
panda properly.

Zoe's mum, Lucy, came walking over
with Auntie Laura.

"Hi, Zoe!" Auntie Laura gave her a big
hug while Lucy greeted the twins.

"Lucy, please could you give her a
quick check-up?" Great-Uncle Horace
asked, holding up the red panda.

Lucy smiled. "Of course!" She peeked
into the red panda's eyes and ears and

listened to her heart with a stethoscope.
"She seems fine,"
Lucy said. "But
I'll give her a
more thorough
check-up after
she's settled in."

Zoe was
excited. "Are
you taking her
to her enclosure
now?" she asked
Great-Uncle
Horace. "Can
I come too?"

"Of course," he
replied. "Just follow me and we'll meet
Stephanie at our red panda's new home."
He waved at the crowd. "I'll see you

all later. Please enjoy your visit to the Rescue Zoo."

"Can we visit her later?" Sam asked.

"Sure," said Zoe. "Let's just give her a little quiet time first, though. The animals can often be a little nervous when they arrive here."

"We can't wait!" said Willow.

Zoe, Meep and Great-Uncle Horace set off along the winding footpath that led through the zoo. The red panda wriggled about excitedly in Great-Uncle Horace's arms, trying to see everything.

"I think she likes the snow," giggled Zoe, as the red panda waved her paws, trying to catch some falling flakes.

"It must remind her of her home in the mountains," said Great-Uncle Horace. "Red pandas also like to live high up in trees, so I'm going to put her in the enclosure next to the penguins."

Zoe smiled. The enclosure next to the penguins had lots of really tall trees. They would be perfect for the red panda to climb in.

When they got to the enclosure, Stephanie, the panda bears' zookeeper, was already inside holding a bundle of bamboo shoots. "Hello Horace, hello Zoe," she called when she saw them. "What's going on?"

"Hello, Stephanie," replied Zoe. "We've got a new type of panda for you."

"You do?" Stephanie ran over, her eyes widening as she caught sight of the red panda. "Oh my goodness," she whispered. "I can't believe it. I've never seen one of these before. Never!"

 23

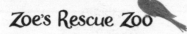

"Really?" said Zoe.

"Red pandas are very rare," Great-Uncle Horace explained.

"And they're not actually related to the panda bear," said Stephanie, her face glowing with excitement. "Although they do look quite similar. And they both love to eat bamboo." She held out a shoot and the red panda began chewing away happily. "There you go," Stephanie cooed. "Aren't you a beauty?"

"Could I hold her for a bit and show her the trees?" asked Zoe.

"Of course." Great-Uncle Horace handed her over. She was so soft and fluffy!

While Great-Uncle Horace and Stephanie talked about getting some more food, Zoe took the red panda over

to a cluster of
trees. She carefully
placed her on the
ground.

"Hello," she
whispered. "I'm Zoe,
and this is Meep." She
unbuttoned her coat
so that Meep could
come out.

The red panda
looked at them both and
squeaked excitedly.

"Hello Ruby, that's
a lovely name." Zoe
smiled. She loved being
able to understand what animals said.

"It's nearly as lovely as Meep," said the
little lemur.

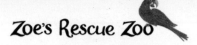
The red panda rolled around in the snow, squealing loudly.

"What's she doing?" asked Meep. "Won't she get freezing?"

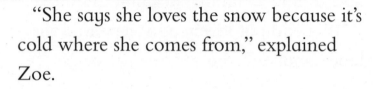

"She says she loves the snow because it's cold where she comes from," explained Zoe.

Ruby wrapped her long tail around her body and chattered excitedly.

"She says her fluffy tail keeps her nice and warm," laughed Zoe.

"Hmm…" Meep looked at his own tail, which was a lot thinner and less fluffy. "I'm not sure my tail would keep me very warm."

"No, but I can." Zoe picked Meep up and tucked him back inside her coat.

Ruby scampered over to the trees and back again, all the time squeaking excitedly.

"You're in my Great-Uncle Horace's Rescue Zoo," explained Zoe. "He's rescued animals from all over the world so you're going to make lots of friends here."

Ruby scampered over to the enclosure fence and looked out. Then she came

racing back and leapt on to Zoe's lap,
chattering away, looking worried.

"Oh, I suppose you'll be alone in your
enclosure, yes," Zoe said. "But you won't
be bored here, trust me! I'll take you to
see the other animals, and you'll see that
you'll have plenty of
friends and fun to
keep you busy!"

Zoe took Ruby back over to Great-Uncle Horace and Stephanie.

"It looks as if you've made a good friend," chuckled Great-Uncle Horace when he saw Ruby snuggled up in Zoe's arms.

"I have. Her name's Ruby," replied Zoe.

"What a nice name," said Stephanie.

"Yes, Zoe always seems to pick just the right names for our animals," said Great-Uncle Horace.

Zoe smiled. If only he knew. She didn't often choose the names at all! The animals usually just told her what they were called when they arrived.

"Please can I show Ruby some of the zoo?" she asked. "I think she'd like to make some friends here to make her feel more at home."

"I don't see why not," replied Great-Uncle Horace. "But keep a tight hold on her. She does like to wriggle!"

"I will."

Zoe made her way over to the enclosure gate and opened it with the silver paw-print pendant around her neck. The pendant had been a gift from Great-Uncle Horace and it opened all of the enclosures in the zoo.

Ruby squeaked so loudly that she made Zoe and Meep jump.

"I know you're excited to see the other animals but you don't need to be so loud about it," Zoe giggled.

"Over there are the penguins," Zoe said, pointing to the lagoon as they made their way outside.

Ruby's ears pricked up and her whiskers

twitched. Zoe tried to tighten her grip but before she could stop her, Ruby had wriggled out of her arms. "No! Come back!" Zoe cried. But it was too late. The little red panda had slipped through a gap in the fence and into the lagoon.

"Uh-oh!" chattered Meep, as Ruby charged into a group of penguins, sending one of them sailing across the ice.

"Wait for me!" Zoe called, running after Ruby. But the little red panda was too fast. By the time Zoe had opened the enclosure gate with her necklace and reached the lagoon Ruby had slipped back out again and raced off along the snowy footpath. "Oh no!" Zoe gasped as Ruby disappeared from view. She looked this way and that, trying to catch a glimpse of red fur.

"Look! Look!" Meep cried, pointing to a set of paw prints on the ground.

Zoe let out a cheer. "Well done, Meep!" She let herself back out of the penguin enclosure and followed the paw prints all the way to the monkeys' enclosure, which was even noisier than usual. All of the monkeys were chattering at the top of their voices about the blur of red fur streaking its way through the top of their trees.

"Her name's Ruby. She's a red panda," explained Zoe, trying to catch her breath. "She's also very fast!" But before she could catch up with Ruby, the little red panda had leapt from the enclosure and was off on her way again, disappearing from view.

"Oh no, not again!" Zoe's heart sank. What was Great-Uncle Horace going to say if she lost Ruby on her very first day at the zoo? And what if she got hurt somehow? Zoe had to find her right away!

Chapter Three
Snowball Fight!

Once again, Zoe followed Ruby's paw
prints in the snow.

"Where do you think she's going this
time?" Meep asked, his head peeping out
from inside Zoe's coat.

"I'm not sure." Zoe caught sight of a
flash of red fur climbing a tree up ahead
of them. "There she is!" Zoe hurried over

to the foot of the tree.

Ruby gave a loud squeak.

"What do you mean, 'that looks like fun'?" Zoe asked. "What are you up to, Ruby?" She gazed up into the branches. Ruby was staring down into the enclosure on the other side of the tree. She gave another loud squeak.

"Oh no!" exclaimed Zoe.

"What is it?" Meep scrambled out of her coat and on to her shoulder to get a better look.

"She's saying she wants to go in that enclosure."

"Which enclosure?"

"The snow leopards' enclosure. No, Ruby, don't!" Zoe called.

Ruby looked down from the branch she was perched on and grunted at Zoe.

"You can't go in there because that's where the snow leopards live," replied Zoe. "You need to come down."

But instead of coming down, Ruby got even more excited.

"Why does she want to see the snow leopards?" asked Meep.

"She says they come from the same part of the world as she does," explained Zoe.

Ruby edged further along the branch, chattering away excitedly.

"I know their enclosure looks really fun," replied Zoe. "But you need to calm down. Please!"

Ruby squeaked again.

Just then, Lila, the mother snow leopard, poked her head out of her cave. Hearing Ruby squeaking, she looked up into the tree.

"Hi, Lila," said Zoe. She really hoped Lila wouldn't be cross about her unexpected visitor. "This is Ruby the red panda. She just moved into the zoo."

Ruby crawled to the very end of the branch. It dipped suddenly, knocking a large lump of snow on to Lila's head!

"Oh no! Ruby!" exclaimed Zoe.

Lila shook the snow from her head and growled. Then she went back inside her cave.

Ruby started running up and down along the branch, chattering at Zoe.

"No, I'm sorry, you can't just explore for a little bit," replied Zoe. Ruby reminded her of her cousin Sam, when he ate too many sweets at his birthday party. He'd started bouncing around all over the place, yelling at the top of his voice. "Lila has four shy little cubs who need to get their sleep."

This time Ruby squealed so loudly Meep almost fell from Zoe's shoulder in shock.

"I don't think it's a good idea to play with them right now," said Zoe. "Why don't you come down and I can show

38

you some more people and animals in the zoo?"

Ruby sighed. To Zoe's relief, she slowly made her way down the tree.

"Don't be sad," said Zoe, scooping her up. Then she had a great idea. "I know, how about we move the snow animal competition to outside your enclosure? Then you'll be able to see everyone decide which animals to build today, and you can watch the judging tomorrow! You couldn't be bored with all that going on, and you'll make loads of new friends. How does that sound?"

Ruby gave a happy little wriggle.

"OK, OK," laughed Zoe. "Stay still."

Zoe headed back to the centre of the zoo with Meep on her shoulder and Ruby in her arms. A small crowd

had gathered outside the café, looking
through the table of props and talking
about which animals they wanted to
build for the contest. It was Saturday, so
children didn't have school and were free
to come to the zoo and compete. Zoe's
cousins, Willow and Sam, were
playing a game of tug-of-war
with a long red scarf. Two
of Zoe's classmates,

Jack and Elliot, were also there, looking through the hats. When they saw Zoe they came running over.

"Hey, Zoe," said Jack. He pointed to Ruby. "Who's this?" As soon as Ruby saw Jack she started to squeak and reach towards him with her paws.

"This is Ruby. She's a red panda, and she's full of energy," laughed Zoe, as she held the wriggly red panda even more tightly.

"Hi Ruby," said Elliot, reaching out his hand for her to sniff. "She's so bouncy!"

"She certainly is." *A little too bouncy,* Zoe thought to herself with a giggle.

Just then Sally emerged from the café. "Good morning, everyone!" she called. "The judge for the snow animal contest will arrive first thing tomorrow, so everyone should decide on their animal and start working right away!"

"Hurray!" cheered Willow. "We're going to make a snow tiger."

"No we're not," called Sam. "We're going to make a snow hippopotamus."

"Would it be OK if we moved the competition a little closer to Ruby's enclosure?" Zoe asked Sally as the twins began to argue. "I think it would really help to keep her occupied if she could see lots of people. She's very friendly."

"So I see," laughed Sally, as Ruby began patting her arm with her paw. "Of course we can."

Everyone gathered up the props and helped move them in front of Ruby's enclosure. "Thanks for looking after her, Zoe," Stephanie called out as she approached. "It looks like she likes it here at the zoo. But perhaps it's about time to get her into her enclosure so she can settle in properly?"

Zoe nodded. But before she could take Ruby into her enclosure, the excited little panda wriggled out of her arms and began to run around in the snow. "Ruby, stop!" Zoe called, but Ruby was too interested in watching the children to listen.

Willow and Sam started building a mound of snow. "I've made a tail," cried Willow.

"That tail's too long for a hippopotamus," said Sam.

"That's because it's for a tiger, silly," replied Willow.

"I'm not silly and this isn't a tiger,"

yelled Sam.

Ruby started scampering around them faster and faster. Then, she rolled on her back, scuffing snow up with her little back legs. A lump of snow hit Sam on the back.

"Hey, don't throw snow at me," he exclaimed, turning to Willow.

"I didn't!" replied Willow.

"Yes, you did." Sam rolled up a snowball and flung it at her.

Ruby shrieked with excitement.

"I know playing with the snow is fun," said Zoe, hurrying over. "But building animals with it is even more fun than

throwing it! Now, let's get to building!"
She picked up Ruby and walked over
to a tree inside her enclosure. "You'll
enjoy watching them from in here too,
I promise," she whispered in the panda's
furry red ear.

Ruby squeaked and climbed up into the
tree. She was calmer but seemed a bit sad.

Zoe sighed. The judge for the Snowy
Paws Award would be arriving the next
day. She really hoped everyone would
calm down and finish getting ready.
Having Ruby at the zoo was a lot of fun
but she certainly was rowdy! And having
Ruby *and* the twins was triple trouble!

Chapter Four
Snow Animal Disaster!

After a long day of decorating and
getting everything in the zoo ready,
Zoe woke up the next morning full of
excitement. It was cold and sunny outside,
the perfect weather for the Snowy Paws
Award judging! After getting dressed,
she fixed breakfast for herself and Meep,
tucked Meep inside her jacket again and

headed over to the café to make a big
batch of hot chocolate. Sally had asked
her to bring some hot drinks for the
children who had come back to the zoo
early to finish building their snow animals
before the judge arrived. She popped a
handful of marshmallows into each of
the drinks, then carefully carried the tray
outside.

"Who wants a hot chocolate?" she
called.

"Yes please!" Elliot grinned. He and
Jack had been busy making a huge snow
elephant but they were having trouble
getting the trunk to stay on.

"Maybe we could turn it into a mouse
instead," sighed Jack as they came over to
get their drinks.

"It would be a giant mouse," giggled

Zoe. She looked over at her cousins. They still hadn't agreed on what animal they were making.

"We can't make a tiger because we can't make it stripy," said Willow.

"Yes we can," replied Sam.

"How?" Willow frowned.

"We could … paint the snow."

"Don't be silly, you can't paint snow."

"I'M NOT SILLY!" yelled Sam.

Ruby was watching all of this from a big tree in her enclosure, its long branches stretching across the wall to the edge of the penguin enclosure. She'd looked bored when Zoe first saw her, but now, hearing the commotion, the red panda scampered down from her tree excitedly.

"Uh-oh!" chattered Meep.

"Willow, Sam, come and get some hot

chocolate," called Zoe. "It's got your
favourite marshmallows in."

To Zoe's relief, the twins stopped
arguing and came running
over to get a drink.
Ruby scampered
over to the
edge of the
enclosure
nearest
to the

children, where there was a big pile of
snow. She started rolling about in it,
throwing snow everywhere and upending
some of the containers of food on the
ground. Everyone stopped what they were
doing to watch and giggle.

"She's so funny," said Willow.

Ruby shook the snow from her fur and
it went flying everywhere. The children
laughed even louder. The little red panda
squeaked with delight at the attention she

was getting and burrowed into a mound of snow. For a couple of seconds there was no sign of her, but then she burst back out.

"Red pandas have so much energy," said Jack.

"This one certainly does," laughed Zoe.

"What on earth is all this noise about?"

They all fell silent at the sound of Mr Pinch's voice. As usual, the zoo manager was dressed in his extra-smart uniform and he was holding a spade.

"Uh-oh!" said Meep, taking cover inside Zoe's coat. Meep didn't really like Mr Pinch as he was always grumpy with him. The truth was, he was grumpy with everyone, and judging by the frown on his face, today was no different.

Mr Pinch glared at Ruby. "What is this

creature? And why is she making such a mess?"

"That is Ruby the red panda," Zoe replied. "She arrived yesterday. She's just having fun in the snow!"

"Ugh! A new animal, now of all times?" spluttered Mr Pinch. He looked around at the half-built snow animals and the props lying on the ground. "The judge for the Snowy Paws Award will be arriving soon. What is she going to think about all this mess?"

I'm sure she won't mind, Zoe thought to herself. *It just shows that everyone is having fun.* "I'm sure once the snow animals are finished it will look great," she said.

Mr Pinch frowned. "Hmm. Well, can you get them finished quickly please? Nobody likes a mess!"

The children all hurried back to their snow animals and carried on building. Mr Pinch started clearing the snow from the footpath leading to the café with his spade.

"We need to make the hippo bigger," Willow said to Sam, adding more snow to their animal.

"No we don't," argued Sam. "We need to make the tiger thinner." And he removed the snow.

"We're not making a tiger!" Willow shouted, trying to put the snow back. But then she lost her footing and went toppling into Sam. Sam went flying backwards – straight into Elliot and Jack's snow elephant! Ruby, who had been playing in her enclosure in the snow next to Jack, squeaked loudly in fright, surprising a girl who was building a snow sloth. The girl stumbled back, knocking the head right off the sloth and on to the ground.

"Oh no!" exclaimed Zoe. Now the zoo looked even messier! She glanced over at Mr Pinch. Thankfully, he was still busy clearing the path and hadn't noticed.

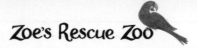

"My sloth's got no head!" cried the little girl.

"Our elephant's got no trunk," sighed Elliot.

"I didn't mean to do it," said Willow, her voice trembling.

"It's OK, don't cry." Zoe hurried over and gave her a hug. "If we all work together, we can help rebuild the animals and clean up the mess."

Sam came over and Zoe wrapped him into the hug too. "I really wanted to win the contest," he said sadly.

"Me too," said Willow. "I told Mum that we would."

Zoe squeezed them tightly. "Auntie Laura will be proud of you no matter what happens. Now let's get these snow animals fixed up, quick!"

Inside her enclosure, Ruby was jumping and playing in the snow again while the children tried to fix their snow animals.

"Sorry, Ruby," Willow said. "We can't play now, we've got to clean up this mess!"

Ruby sighed and slowly climbed up her tree once more. As Zoe and Meep helped the others rebuild their snow animals, Ruby gave encouraging squeaks from high in the branches.

Zoe worked as fast as she could, helping the little girl rebuild her sloth's head. She really hoped they'd get it all done in time. She'd had no idea the Snowy Paws Award would be quite so tiring!

Chapter Five
Showing Off

The children were all happily rebuilding their snow animals when Great-Uncle Horace and Zoe's mum Lucy came hurrying over.

"The judge is about to arrive," said Lucy.

"But the Zoo isn't nearly tidy enough!" exclaimed Mr Pinch, striding over, holding his spade. "There's still snow all over the place."

"It is the *Snowy* Paws Award," chuckled Great-Uncle Horace. "I think the snow looks lovely. Now, let's go and meet the judge and take her to see the special winter animal exhibits. Zoe, would you like to come too? You know so much about the zoo. I'm sure you'll be able to tell her some wonderful facts about the animals. We want to make sure she has the best day out ever."

"Oh, yes please!" Zoe tucked Meep into her coat and hurried over.

"I don't really see how a child would know more about the animals than me. *I* am the zoo manager," grumbled Mr Pinch.

"Now, now, Mr Pinch, the more the

merrier," said Great-Uncle Horace, giving Zoe a wink.

Zoe tried not to giggle. It was more like "the more the grumpier" when it came to Mr Pinch. But she knew that Mr Pinch was only so grumpy because he cared about the zoo and wanted them to win.

As they reached the zoo gates Zoe saw a rather stern looking woman holding a clipboard. She had short grey hair and she was wearing a tightly buttoned up coat, a neat scarf and very shiny shoes.

Zoe's heart sank a little. The judge didn't look very friendly. Zoe hoped she'd like the snowy activities and give them a good score.

"Hello, I'm Mrs Price," said the judge.

"Welcome to the Rescue Zoo." Great-Uncle Horace took Mrs Price's hand and

60

gave it a hearty shake. "This is my niece Lucy, the zoo vet, and her daughter Zoe. And this is Mr Pinch, the zoo manager."

"Very pleased to meet you," said Mrs Price, shaking each of their hands. When she got to Zoe, Meep gave a welcoming chirp from inside her coat. "Oh my goodness!" Mrs Price took a step back in shock.

"This is my mouse lemur, Meep," explained Zoe. "He's my best friend and he goes everywhere with me."

"Unfortunately," muttered Mr Pinch.

"I see," said Mrs Price, writing something on her clipboard. Zoe hoped she wasn't giving the zoo a bad mark already!

"Let the tour begin," announced Great-Uncle Horace.

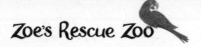
The first stop on the tour was the polar bears' enclosure.

"There's Snowy," said Great-Uncle Horace, as they gathered outside the enclosure. The polar bear was digging away happily inside a gravel pit.

"Great-Uncle Horace rescued Snowy when she was just a baby," said Zoe.

"Is that so?" replied Mrs Price. "She looks as if she's really settled in."

"Oh she has," said Zoe. "The pit she's digging in was just added to her enclosure a little while ago."

"Yes, as an enrichment activity," Great-Uncle Horace added. "Enrichment activities help animals feel at home and keep them busy."

Mrs Price nodded.

"Did you know that polar bears' fur used to be brown but it became white so they could camouflage themselves in the snow?" Zoe continued.

"I did not know that." Mrs Price's mouth curled upwards into a slight smile.

"And they can swim for two hundred miles."

"Goodness me! That's very interesting." Mrs Price's smile grew bigger and Zoe relaxed a little.

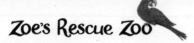

"Zoe and I made a poster for the exhibit." Lucy pointed to a colourful poster on the enclosure wall. "It's got lots of other fun facts about polar bears on it."

Mrs Price went over to read the poster, then she wrote something on her clipboard. "Where to next?" she asked.

"The next enclosure belongs to the snow leopards," replied Mr Pinch. He led her along the freshly cleared footpath.

"I love the decorations you've put up," Mrs Price said, gesturing toward the pretty little blue lights in the trees, the garlands hung across the signs, and the paw-print cutouts placed along the footpath. "They're very creative."

"Yes, our volunteers did a superb job with them," remarked Great-Uncle Horace.

"And it's all very neat and tidy," Mrs
Price added.

"Oh, thank you!" exclaimed Mr Pinch.

65

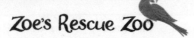

Zoe looked at Lucy and raised her eyebrows. Mr Pinch and Mrs Price seemed to have a lot in common. She really hoped Mrs Price wouldn't think that the rest of the zoo was too messy.

When they got to the snow leopards' enclosure the cubs had finished their nap and were tumbling about in the snow outside their cave. Two of them came scampering over to the wall of the enclosure to say hello.

"This is Holly and Ivy," said Zoe.

"They certainly look very excited to see you," said Mrs Price, as the two cubs started to play fight in the snow.

Zoe grinned. "I think they're excited to see the snow too. Did you know that snow leopards have extra big paws to help them walk in the snow?"

"No, I didn't," replied Mrs Price.

"All that extra fur helps keep their toes warm too," added Lucy.

"Well, this is most interesting," said Mrs Price.

"OK, next stop, the penguins," announced Great-Uncle Horace.

"Oh, I do love penguins," said Mrs Price.

"Me too." Mr Pinch nodded. "Very tidy creatures."

Mrs Price smiled and Zoe's heart sank. The judge really did hate mess as much as Mr Pinch. What would she think when she saw how messy the snow animal competition was?

As they reached the penguin enclosure, two of the younger penguins, Pip and Percy, started sliding around on the ice on their tummies. Zoe knew they were

putting on a dance show for their special visitor.

"Oh, how lovely," said Mrs Price.

Behind them, the children were putting the finishing touches to their snow animals. All the mess had gone now, thankfully. Zoe smiled. Everything was going really well. Mrs Price seemed to like the zoo and even Mr Pinch seemed almost happy. But then she heard a loud squeak from high above.

"Uh-oh," Meep chattered from inside Zoe's coat.

Uh-oh, thought Zoe, as she looked up to see Ruby perched on a long tree branch that stretched from her enclosure over to the edge of the penguin enclosure. A group of penguins had gathered by the fence and were looking up at her. Zoe listened hard to Ruby's squeaks and her heart sank. The little red panda was showing off to the penguins that she could dance too – along the branch with her eyes closed!

"Ruby, don't!" cried Zoe. "That's dangerous!"

But she was too late. Zoe watched in horror as Ruby lost her footing – and fell straight into the penguins' enclosure!

Chapter Six
Ruby Makes a Friend

Ruby landed on the ice with a thud. The penguins who had been dancing went skidding off to the side. A loud cracking noise filled the air.

"What's that sound?" asked Mrs Price.

"It's the ice," replied Zoe, her heart pounding. What if Ruby fell into the icy water? She wasn't sure if red pandas could swim!

There was another loud crack as Ruby tried to get on to her paws but slipped and slid back down again.

"Don't move, Ruby, I'm coming!" Zoe ran over to the enclosure entrance and felt for the paw-print pendant around her neck. But before she could go inside some of the penguins started gliding over the ice to Ruby. Zoe held her breath as she watched. She really hoped the ice wouldn't break. Poor Ruby whimpered helplessly. Very slowly and very carefully, the penguins guided the red panda to the safety of the snowy shore.

Lucy rushed into the enclosure. Ruby might be hurt! Everyone, including Mrs Price, looked on with worried eyes. But Ruby had already started to squirm again and as Lucy checked her over, she looked like she was going to be OK.

Zoe noticed that Pip, the youngest penguin, looked really sad. She followed Lucy into the enclosure with Meep still tucked in her coat, and went over to the penguins. "Well done for saving her," she whispered to them. "But what's the matter, Pip?"

The little penguin gave a sad squawk.

"I'm sorry Ruby stopped your show," said Zoe, "but I don't think it's made the judge cross." She glanced outside the enclosure. Mrs Price was busy chatting away to Mr Pinch and Great-Uncle Horace. "I think you should carry on dancing."

Pip squawked hopefully.

"Yes, I don't think the judge will mind

the break at all." Zoe sighed. She really hoped this was true.

The penguins got on with their show for Mrs Price and Zoe hurried over to her mum.

"How's Ruby?"

"She's OK. No broken bones thankfully. She's just a little shocked."

"I'm not surprised." Zoe stroked the red panda's head. "Shall I put her back in her enclosure?"

Lucy nodded. "Yes please."

Zoe let Meep out of her coat and carefully carried Ruby back outside.

"How is she?" Mrs Price called over.

"She's OK," replied Zoe, trying to ignore Mr Pinch's glare.

She quickly let herself into Ruby's enclosure and went behind the trees so they couldn't be seen. Meep scampered along behind them.

"Ruby, why did you do that?" asked Zoe. "You could have been really hurt. You could have fallen through the ice."

Ruby hung her head and huffed sadly.

"Oh Ruby." Zoe cuddled her tightly. "I understand it's boring to be all alone in your enclosure. You just wanted to be part of the show with the penguins."

Ruby nuzzled into her and chirped again.

"I know you like playing with your new friends, but there are much less rowdy ways to have fun!"

"Yes," chattered Meep. "You could give other animals food. Food is the most fun thing ever!"

"All Meep ever thinks about is food,"

joked Zoe.

"No, I don't!" The little mouse lemur puffed up his chest crossly. "I don't think of food when I'm asleep ... apart from when I dream about it," he added.

Ruby ran off behind a tree and came back with a bamboo shoot. She dropped it on the floor in front of Meep.

"Ah, look, she's given you a present," said Zoe.

Meep chattered excitedly and Ruby gave a happy squeak.

"There, see, you've made a friend without doing anything silly," said Zoe.

Ruby nodded.

"If you could just stay in your enclosure for now, I promise that after the judge has gone, I'll try to help you find more things to do. Does that sound all right?"

Ruby squeaked yes.

"Thank you." Zoe stroked Ruby's fur. "I'd better go and see how the snow animal contest is going. We'll be back soon."

Zoe and Meep got back to the others just as the penguins were finishing their show. Will, their keeper, came out of his shed holding a bucket. The penguins gathered round as he threw them handfuls of krill to say well done.

Mrs Price glanced over to Ruby's enclosure. Then she wrote something on her clipboard. She seemed very serious. Zoe's heart sank. What if Pip had been right? What if Ruby interrupting the penguins' show had made them lose the Snowy Paws Award?

Chapter Seven
Flying Hats and Scarves

Mrs Price finished writing and pointed to the area in front of the café. "What are those children doing?"

"Oh, you don't want to see them," said Mr Pinch hastily. "You know how messy children can be."

"They're having a snow animal-making contest," said Zoe, ignoring Mr Pinch's

79

frown. "Would you like to watch?"

"Yes, please." Mrs Price nodded.

"But you haven't seen all of the neat and tidy parts of the zoo," spluttered Mr Pinch. "And the rest of the splendid decorations."

"I'm sure I'll get to see them eventually," replied Mrs Price.

As Zoe led the judge over to the café, she hoped Willow and Sam had stopped arguing. The last thing they needed was anything else going wrong. At least Ruby was now safe and calm inside her enclosure. Zoe glanced over. The red panda was perched high in a tree, munching on a bamboo shoot and watching the children.

Mrs Price headed over to Elliot and Jack. "Hello young men, what's that you're building?"

"It's an elephant," replied Elliot proudly.

"It took us ages to get its trunk right," said Jack.

"I think it's marvellous," said Mrs Price.

Zoe grinned. Mrs Price was right. The trunk was great. It was huge and curved right down to the ground.

"Now we just need to choose a scarf for our elephant to wear," said Elliot, pointing to the pile of props on the ground.

While Jack and Elliot showed Mrs Price the props, Zoe went over to her cousins. There was still a big heap of snow in front of them.

"It doesn't look like a hippo," whispered Sam.

"Well it doesn't look like a tiger either," replied Willow crossly.

 81

Zoe was very relieved that Mrs Price was still busy talking to Jack and Elliot. "Come on you two," she said to the twins. "There must be an animal you both want to make."

"But tigers are so tough and cool," said Sam.

"Yeah, but hippos are unique!" said Willow. "No one else would think of making one!"

"Why don't you make something completely different?" suggested Zoe.

Sam looked thoughtful. "How about a snow snake?"

"No, snow snakes are boring," said Willow.

Zoe sighed and shook her head. She wondered if the twins would ever agree on something! A sudden gust of wind blew through the zoo and Zoe shivered. She hoped Sally would make some more of her delicious hot chocolate soon. It was getting really chilly.

Great-Uncle Horace went and stood in front of the café. "Attention everyone, it's time to judge the Snow Animal Contest."

The crowd fell silent. Even Willow and Sam stopped arguing.

Great-Uncle Horace smiled at them all. "You've all worked very hard on your snow animals. Mrs Price, I was wondering if you would do the honours?"

"I would love to," replied Mrs Price.

Zoe held her breath as the judge inspected each of the snow animals.

"OK, I have made my decision," Mrs Price said. "The winner is … this magnificent snow elephant!"

"Yes!" cheered Elliot.

"We won!" cried Jack.

Zoe ran over to congratulate them. But before she could say a word, another icy blast blew through the zoo. The children gasped as some of the props were whipped up into the air and into the biggest tree in the whole zoo, which stood

right at the
edge of Ruby's enclosure.
"Oh no!" cried Elliot as the
scarf he'd put around the snow
elephant's neck was sent flying.
"My snow fox has lost his
hat," cried another boy.

A little girl started to cry.
"My snow zebra will be cold
without his hat on."
"Of course he'll be cold, he's made
of snow," Meep chattered.
Zoe shushed him and went over
to give the girl a hug. "Don't
worry, we'll get your
zebra's hat back."

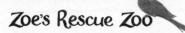

"How?" sobbed the little girl. "It's stuck in that tree."

Zoe looked over to the tree-top. It was covered in hats and scarves. She'd thought the worst was over after the penguins rescued Ruby, but things just kept on going wrong!

Another gust of wind whipped around them.

"My scarf!" cried Mrs Price as her scarf was pulled from her neck by the wind and flew up into the tree as well.

"Can't someone climb up the tree and get them?" said Jack.

"I'll climb it," said Elliot.

"No, no, no," said Great-Uncle Horace. "It's far too high and the branches aren't strong enough to hold a person."

Zoe felt her heart sinking. *There's no way*

we will win if Mrs Price's scarf is stuck up there.

Suddenly, Zoe saw a flash of red fur streak through the tree. "Oh no," she whispered as she watched Ruby scampering higher and higher. What was the lively red panda going to do this time?

Everyone watched as Ruby bounced around the branches. She leapt, grabbed one of the hats in her paws and put it on her head. She jumped to the next branch and picked up another hat. Then another, and then a scarf. The tree was swaying beneath her paws and snow was showering down on to the ground. Balancing the hats and scarf, Ruby carefully made her way back down the tree.

"She's stealing my snow zebra's hat," sniffed the little girl.

"I don't think she's
stealing it," Zoe grinned. "I
think she's saving it."

And sure enough, the little red
panda came scampering over
to the enclosure gate. She looked
very funny dressed up so warmly.
All the children started laughing.
Zoe felt for the paw-print
pendant around her neck and

opened the enclosure gate. Ruby came scampering out. Willow unwrapped Mrs Price's scarf and handed it back to her. As soon as the hats and scarf were collected, Ruby scampered back up into the tree to get more. Back and forth she went, until all the props were out of the tree. The children cheered.

"Now my snow zebra won't be cold!" the little girl said, smiling.

Once Ruby was done, Zoe picked her up and gave her a hug.

Ruby grunted anxiously.

"It's OK," Zoe whispered. "You didn't mess up anything with your little trick – you made everything better! It was very kind of you to rescue the props." She only hoped that Mrs Price didn't mind what had happened. She looked over at the judge nervously. She looked very serious. Zoe felt really sad. *Looks like we've lost the Snowy Paws Award...*

Chapter Eight
And the Winner is...

Everyone fell silent as Mrs Price got ready
to speak. Her serious expression softened.
She looked like she had made a decision.
"What a wonderful zoo this is," she said.
She smiled at Ruby. "And what a lively
red panda. Thank you for putting on such
a great show." Mrs Price began to clap
and everyone joined in – even Mr Pinch!

91

"You picked the perfect time to be rowdy after all," Zoe whispered as she put Ruby on the ground.

The little red panda bounced for joy on the snow.

Mrs Price looked down at her clipboard. "And now for the results of the Snowy Paws Award."

Zoe's heart thudded. She really hoped they'd done enough to win!

"I was very impressed by the wonderful wintry decorations in the Rescue Zoo," Mrs Price continued. "And the tidy footpaths as well. Clearing the snow from them made it so much easier for the guests to get around."

Mr Pinch's normal frown turned into a huge grin. Zoe had never seen him looking so happy!

"And the zoo is so well-organized too," said Mrs Price. "So that even in the winter, there's much to look at."

Mr Pinch's smile grew even bigger.

"You have done a wonderful job showcasing the special winter animals and teaching visitors all about them."

Zoe hugged Meep to her.

"And the animals themselves are clearly very happy and well cared for here, no matter what the weather!"

Ruby, who was still rolling around on the ground, gave an excited squeak. Everyone started laughing.

"I loved finding out all of the interesting facts about the winter animals," said Mrs Price. "Thank you very much, Zoe."

Zoe smiled proudly.

Great-Uncle Horace patted her on the

back. "Well done, Zoe."

"I especially liked watching the
penguins dancing on the ice." Mrs Price
chuckled. "But I think my favourite
moment has to be the red panda rescuing
the hats and scarves!"

Everyone started laughing again and
Ruby squeaked excitedly.

"This is the most fun zoo I've ever
been to," continued Mrs Price. "I've had
the most wonderful wintry day out. So,
without further ado, I declare the Rescue
Zoo the winner of the Snowy Paws
Award!"

The crowd all began to cheer.

Mrs Price took a silver trophy from
her bag. It had a paw print on the front.
She handed the trophy to Great-Uncle
Horace.

"So you didn't mind it when things got messy?" asked Zoe, hardly able to believe what she'd just heard.

"Of course not," replied Mrs Price. "A little mess is the sign of fun."

Zoe wanted to jump up and down she was so happy.

Mr Pinch muttered something under his breath but he kept on smiling.

"Thank you very much!" exclaimed Great-Uncle Horace. "And thank you to everyone who has worked so hard to help us win. Thank you to the keepers who take such good care of our animals. And thank you to Mr Pinch for keeping the footpaths so neat and tidy."

"Well, somebody has to," Mr Pinch muttered, but at least he was still smiling.

"And to say thank you, I'd like to buy hot chocolates for everybody!" called Great-Uncle Horace.

The crowd cheered and headed into the café.

Zoe noticed Ruby standing on top of

a mound of snow. Her tail had drooped between her legs and she looked really sad.

"What's the matter, Ruby?"

The little red panda gave a sad squeak.

"Why is she sad?" asked Meep.

"She doesn't want everyone to go. She wants something to do," explained Zoe. "She was happy when she was taking part in all the activities, but now she's going to be bored and alone again." Then she had a great idea. She picked Ruby up. "I'm going to take you to see my mum," explained Zoe.

She hurried over to Lucy, who was outside the café.

"Hi, Mum. You know how you're planning to give Ruby a more thorough check-up?"

"Yes." Lucy nodded.

"I was just wondering if you could give Ruby her check-up now – please."

"Oh, I suppose I'd meant to do that today, but with all the excitement I haven't had time," Lucy said. "But why right now, Zoe?"

"It's really important. I need to do something while you've got Ruby," she whispered in Lucy's ear.

"Well, the zoo hospital is pretty quiet at the moment." Lucy nodded. "OK, love, give her to me."

Zoe gave a sigh of relief as Lucy took

the little red panda. "Thank you. And –
er – can you take a long time doing the
check-up?" she whispered.

Lucy looked even more puzzled. "What
are you up to, Zoe?"

"It's a secret," replied Zoe. "I want to
do something to surprise Ruby," she
whispered.

"Ah, I see." Lucy grinned. "OK, one
extra-long check-up coming up!"

Lucy headed off to the zoo hospital
with Ruby.

Meep bounced up and down chattering
away. "What's the secret? What's the
secret? Please tell me."

"I think Ruby needs more enrichment,"
said Zoe.

"What's enrichment? Is it something to
eat?" chattered Meep.

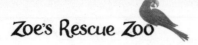

"No!" laughed Zoe. "Although
sometimes it can be." She picked up the
little lemur. "It's when you give animals
fun and interesting things to do – that's
what Great-Uncle Horace taught me. I'm
going to see if we can put some things in

Ruby's enclosure to keep her busy. She's got so much energy, and this way she'll never be bored again. Come on, we need to find Stephanie!"

Chapter Nine
A Lovely Surprise

Zoe hurried past Willow and Sam, who were *still* working on their snow animal! She spotted Stephanie coming out of the café holding a hot chocolate and hurried over.

"Hi Stephanie. Ruby's just gone for her check-up. Could we give her a lovely surprise when she gets back?"

"That sounds exciting." Stephanie grinned. "Tell me more."

So Zoe told Stephanie all about her plan to fill Ruby's enclosure with enrichment activities.

"I think that's an excellent idea," said Stephanie. "You're going to make a great zookeeper one day, Zoe."

"Thank you." Zoe blushed.

"Let's go to the storage shed and see what we can find," said Stephanie.

Inside the shed they found all kinds of fun things for Ruby. Ladders for her to climb, rope and barrels and a piece of fabric for her to play with, and boxes for her to explore. Zoe and Stephanie piled them all up on the ground outside.

"Uh-oh," squeaked Meep, who was standing on top of one of the barrels.

"What's all this mess? What's going on?" barked Mr Pinch as he marched up the footpath towards them.

"We're making a lovely surprise for Ruby," explained Zoe.

"A lovely surprise? It looks more like a nasty shock to me!" snapped Mr Pinch.

"Don't worry, Mr Pinch," said Stephanie. "It's not staying here. We're taking these things to Ruby's enclosure for her to play with."

"It's called enrichment," said Zoe.

"It's called a mess," said Mr Pinch.

"Maybe you could help us carry it to her enclosure," suggested Stephanie. "That way we'll clear it all out of the way a lot faster." She grinned at Zoe.

"Yes. You're so good at tidying things," said Zoe.

"Hmm, that is true. After all, I did just win an award for the tidiest zoo," replied Mr Pinch.

"I thought it was called the Snowy Paws Award," said Stephanie.

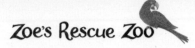
"Yes, but the judge said the Rescue Zoo won at least partly because it was so tidy." Mr Pinch picked up one of the ladders. "Come on then, let's get this cleared up."

Once they'd moved everything into Ruby's enclosure, Zoe helped Stephanie put it all into place.

"Shall we put some fruit in the boxes for Ruby to find?" she suggested.

"Great idea," agreed Stephanie.

Meep seemed very excited about the surprise too, running round in a circle chasing his tail.

Zoe fetched some blueberries from the enclosure shed. She gave a handful to Meep before putting the rest in a couple of the boxes. She filled the rest of the boxes with some of the props that hadn't been used in the snow animal

contest. Then she and Stephanie made
a hammock from the rope and piece of
fabric and hung it between the trees. Just
as they were putting the finishing touches
to the enclosure, Meep chattered loudly.
Lucy and Ruby were coming back! Zoe
hurried out to meet them.

"Hello Ruby, I've got a surprise for
you." She took the little red panda from
Lucy.

"What have you been up to?" asked
Lucy.

"Come and see."

Zoe took Ruby inside the enclosure and
put her down on the ground. As soon as
the little red panda saw the ladders and
barrels and boxes she began to squeak.

"Go and explore," said Zoe.

She watched as Ruby scampered up

a ladder into a tree. Then she ran back
down again and looked inside one of
the boxes. A crowd of people started
gathering outside the enclosure to see
what was happening.

"Oh look, she's got things to play with,"
said Jack.

"Cool ladder!" said Elliot.

They all laughed as Ruby pulled a
hat from a box and put it on her head.

Ruby ran over to the fence and squeaked at the crowd. Everyone cheered, which made Ruby even more excited. As she scampered over to the hammock Zoe gave a sigh of relief. Now Ruby had a safe place to be silly *and* attract lots of the attention that she loved. Not only that, as a newly arrived animal, loads more visitors would surely come to zoo to meet her – even in the snow!

Ruby hopped into the hammock and started swinging back and forth.

The crowd cheered even louder.

Zoe picked Meep up and slipped out of the enclosure. The only people who weren't watching Ruby were Willow and Sam. They were *still* working on their snow animal! Zoe went over to see how they were doing.

"Hi, Zoe, we've made our snow animal," said Willow.

They stood back and Zoe saw that they had made a pretty little red panda, with three hats balanced on its head.

"It's brilliant!" said Zoe.

The twins beamed at her.

"It looks a bit silly," said Sam, pointing at the hats.

"Just like Ruby," giggled Willow.

"You're right. It looks exactly like Ruby." Zoe grinned. "Come on, let's go and get a hot chocolate with marshmallows."

"Yay!" cheered the twins.

"I like pink marshmallows best," said Sam as they made their way over to the café.

"No, white marshmallows are the best," said Willow.

As the twins started arguing again Zoe couldn't help grinning. Her cousins were as rowdy as Ruby. But they were just as cute too. She wondered if the next animal Great-Uncle Horace rescued would be just as lively. She couldn't wait to find out!

If you enjoyed Ruby's story,
look out for:

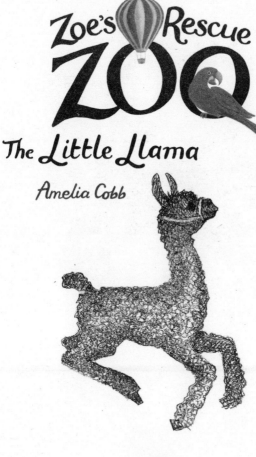

Zoe's Rescue Zoo

The Little Llama

Amelia Cobb

nosy
crow

Chapter One
Very Special Guests

Zoe Parker finished her packed lunch and rushed out into the playground.

"Is it snowing yet?" called her friend Priti from behind her.

"No!" sighed Zoe. The weather forecast had been saying it might snow all week but so far there hadn't been a single flake, despite it being freezing cold. Zoe and her friends were so excited about playing in the snow! Still, Zoe did have something to look forward to. This afternoon her Great-Uncle Horace was coming to give a talk at her school. It was almost time for the school's big winter show and Great-Uncle Horace had agreed to help them with it this year!

Zoe's Great-Uncle Horace was a famous explorer and he travelled all over the world rescuing animals who were lost, injured or endangered. He brought the animals back to live at the Rescue Zoo. Zoe lived at the zoo too, with her mum, Lucy, who was the zoo vet.

"It's so cold!" said Zoe's friend Jack, coming out to join the girls. "Shall we play chase to warm up?"

"Good idea!" grinned Zoe.

But before they could begin their game she heard the sound of a car horn playing a musical tune. Zoe's eyes sparkled. There was only one car horn she knew that sounded like that and it belonged to Great-Uncle Horace! She spun round to face the school gates. Sure enough, Great-Uncle Horace's cherry-red car was pulling up outside.

"It's my great-uncle!" she cried.

"Cool car!" exclaimed Priti.

Great-Uncle Horace's car was a convertible, which meant that the roof could come down. But the roof wasn't down today because it was far too cold. A wooden trailer was attached to the back of the car. Zoe felt butterflies flutter in her tummy. Great-Uncle Horace usually used the trailer to transport animals in. Had he brought an animal with him to *school*?

"Come on, let's go and see him!" said Zoe, and she and her friends hurried over to the school gates.

The school caretaker opened the gates and Great-Uncle Horace drove inside and parked next to the playing field.

"Zoe, my dear!" he cried as he got out of the car. "It's so wonderful to see you. Brrrr, it's a bit chilly though!"

"It's so good to see you too!" said Zoe, giving him a big hug. Then she heard a weird humming sound coming from the trailer.

"What's in the trailer?" she asked.

"A special guest," replied Great-Uncle Horace with a twinkle in his eyes. "I've just collected her, so I thought I'd bring her along to join in the fun!"

"I thought *you* were the special guest."
Zoe giggled.

"Well, yes, I suppose I am." Great-Uncle
Horace grinned. "But this guest is even
more special!"

Zoe's Rescue Zoo

**Look out for more
amazing animal adventures
at the Rescue Zoo!**

The Rescue Princesses

Look out for another AMAZING series from Nosy Crow!

Friendship, animals and
secret royal adventures!